NICKELODEON®

RUGRATS™

Oh, Brother!

by Luke David

illustrated by Louie del Carmen and James Peters

Simon Spotlight/Nickelodeon

Based on the TV series *Rugrats*® created by Arlene Klasky, Gabor Csupo, and Paul Germain as seen on NICKELODEON®

SIMON SPOTLIGHT
An imprint of Simon & Schuster Children's Publishing Division
1230 Avenue of the Americas
New York, NY 10020

This edition published by Grolier Books.
Grolier Books is a division of Grolier Enterprises, Inc.

ISBN 0-7172-8911-7

Tommy smiled. He had built a tall block tower all by himself. Tommy was very proud.

Then his baby brother, Dil, swiped the top block away. "Look at Dil grab," exclaimed their mother Didi. "He's mastering fine motor control. It's wonderful."

Dil swiped another block. The tower came tumbling down. Tommy was annoyed.

"I don't remember Tommy using such fine hand-eye motor coordination until he was much older," said Stu, their father.

Didi gave a quick nod. "And see how well Dil can hold up his head."

"Amazing!" agreed Chuckie's dad, Chas.

Tommy looked at Dil. Then he toddled over to Chuckie. "I can hold up my head," whispered Tommy. "And you can too, Chuckie. We big babies are just as good as little ones. At least I think we are. Don't you, Chuckie?"

"Well, I don't know, Tommy. The growed-ups seem to think your baby brother is pretty special," answered Chuckie. "It's Dil, Dil, Dil all the time!"

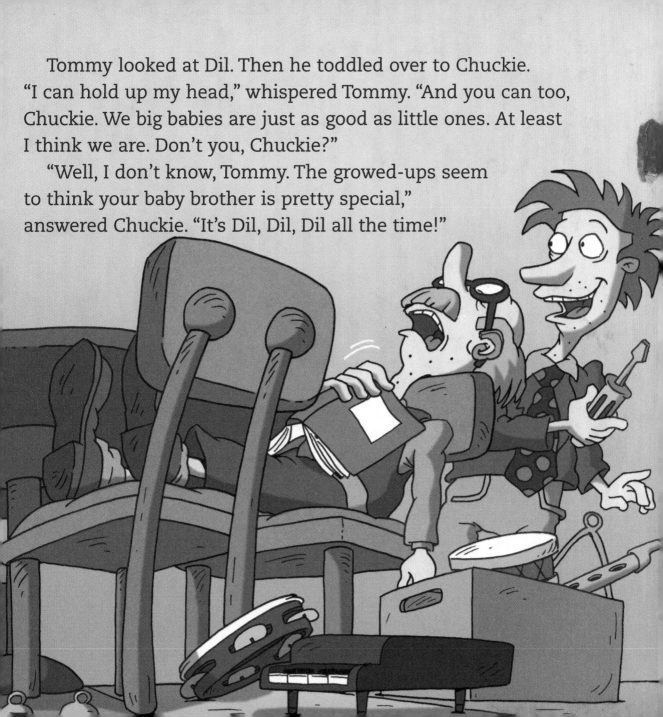

"But the growed-ups love us, too, Chuckie," replied Tommy.
"I'm sure of it!"

Just then Dil put his foot in his mouth.

"Wow!" said Stu. "Now *that's* coordination. Yep, Dil's a
chip off the old block."

"Oh, Stu!" said Didi. "Dil is adorable."

"If Dil is a doorbell, I don't see why we can't be doorbells too!" Tommy said as he gave Chuckie some finger cymbals. "Maybe then the growed-ups will think we're great too."

Then Tommy dug some bells out of the music crate for himself. *Ting-a-ling-a-ling! Ding-ding-ding!* They rang the cymbals and the bells all at once.

Didi plugged her ears. "Boys!" she called. "Please stop that racket."

Tommy looked sad. Dil blew a bubble with his drool.

"No doubt about it," said Chas as he coochie-cooed Dil under the chin, "little babies are delightful."

"If Dil is light-full," said Chuckie, "we can be light-full too. C'mon, Tommy!"

So Tommy and Chuckie went to get flashlights.

"Yowee, Chuckie!" complained his dad. "You're shining that flashlight right in my eyes. Please turn it off."

Now Chuckie was sad too. But Didi didn't notice. She said, "You'll remember, Chas, from when Chuckie was tiny, that caring for an infant is not always easy . . ."

Dil interrupted. He bubbered his lips with his finger. "Bubber-bubber-bubber." Then he smiled at his mom.

Didi beamed. She gave Dil a quick kiss. "Still, Dil certainly can be angelic."

"Angelica!" said Tommy. "Now they think Dil is like Angelica! What's so good about her anyway?"

"Nothing," answered Chuckie. "Angelica is mean and she's naughty."

"Eggs-actly, Chuckie!" said Tommy. "But if the growed-ups want more Angelica, that's what we'll give them!"

Didi brought the kids into the living room.

"Okay, Chuckie," whispered Tommy. "If we're going to be like Angelica, we've got to act like Angelica."

"I don't know, Tommy," answered Chuckie.

"Well, I do!" said Tommy. "If Angelica wanted the growed-ups to pay attention to her instead of Dil, she'd just hide the baby. Watch!"

Dil yanked the blankie off his head. He opened his mouth wide and screamed, "WAAAAAAAAGH!"

Didi and Chas dropped what they were doing. Neither knew how to stop Dil from crying.

"I'll get his Binky," said Chas. He ran upstairs.

"I'll get his bottle," said Didi. She dashed into the kitchen.

"WAAAAAAAAGH!" Dil kept wailing.

"See what you get for being like Angelica, Tommy?" said Chuckie. "What do we do now? How can we get Dil to stop crying?"

"Maybe we should go back to being our regular selves," said Tommy. He smiled at his baby brother. Then Tommy picked up a toy train. "Choo-choo-choo-choo!" He drove it around Dil's cushion. "Choo-choo-choo-choo!"

Chuckie made funny faces. Dil cried a little less.
Tommy played peekaboo with Dil. Dil dried his eyes.
Then he started to giggle.

Didi came back with Dil's bottle and Chas came back with his Binky. But Dil was already okay.

This time Didi scooped up Tommy. She looked down at Dil. "Well, Dil," she said. "One thing is certain—you're *very* lucky to have a big brother like Tommy."

"And a friend like Chuckie," added Chas, and he gave Chuckie a big hug too.

THE END

Now flip the book over to start another Rugrats adventure.